The Best Fairy Tales of Andersen

The Princess and the Pea	1
Thumbelina	25
The Little Mermaid	49
The Emperor's New Clothes	73
The Steadfast Tin Soldier	97
The Wild Swans	121
The Nightingale	145
The Ugly Duckling	169
The Red Shoes	193
The Little Match Girl	217

The Princess and the Pea

Once upon a time there lived a handsome prince in a large castle. His parents, the king and queen of the country, wanted their son to become the new ruler and watch over all of their kingdom. This could only happen if the prince married a princess, but the girl would have to be a genuine princess.

So the prince set off to find his princess. He travelled far and wide, all around the country and all around the world, in his search to find the right girl.

But no matter how much he journeyed, how many countries and places he visited, and how far he travelled, nowhere could he find the princess he wanted.

Wherever the young prince went, there were more than enough princesses to be found, but he soon discovered that it was exceedingly difficult for him to tell whether or not they were real ones. There always seemed to be something about them that was not quite as it should be.

Sometimes they were too tall, sometimes they were too short. Sometimes they were too young, sometimes they were too old. Sometimes they had a terrible haircut or a horrible way of dressing!

The prince carried on searching and searching, but it felt as though his search was in vain. For no matter how far he ventured and no matter how hard he tried, he found fault with every single girl he found.

So, feeling defeated and very sad, the young prince returned again to his homeland and his castle. He was so disappointed, for he would have liked very much to have found a genuine princess. Someone who would make him happy. Someone who would make him laugh, and who he could marry and spend the rest of his life with.

'I do so wish that he would meet someone and settle down', sighed the king, 'but even if he does, how are we ever going to be sure that she is a real princess?' The king and queen were very concerned for their son, but the queen reassured her husband: 'Leave that to me. When he finds the girl, I know how to tell for certain'.

One night some time later, a terrible storm raged all around the kingdom and the castle. There were crashes of thunder and flashes of lightning, and rain poured down from the sky in great torrents.

Suddenly, in the very middle of the storm, a knocking was heard at the castle gates. 'My goodness. Who could be up at so late an hour, wandering around in such terrible weather?' asked the king. 'Some poor fellow must be outside in this storm. We really must let him in to get warm and dry'.

So the old king went down through the castle to open the gates and see for himself who it could possibly be.

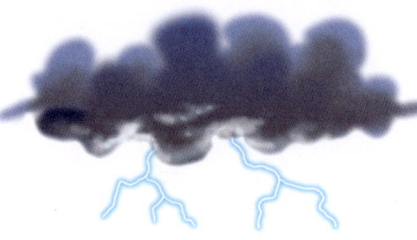The old king opened the castle gates, and to his great surprise, in front of him stood a young girl. But, goodness gracious! What a terrible state the rain and the wind had made her look.

Water ran down from her hair and clothes. It poured down into the toes of her shoes and out again at the heels. The poor old king could hardly believe his eyes.

'I am so very sorry to trouble you', said the young girl. 'My carriage overturned and I was forced to go in search of shelter. And you would be truly surprised to find out just how few people are ready to help a real princess knocking at their door at night in the midst of a storm like this!'

They gave the girl some dry clothes and offered her a place to sleep during the stormy night.

When the prince saw the girl all dressed up, he immediately fell in love with her. 'This must be the princess I have been looking for all this time', thought the prince, 'but how can I know for sure that she is a real princess?'

The king and the queen went to another room and discussed how to solve the question. 'Well, we'll soon find that out', said the queen. 'If she is a real princess, as she claims, then she must surely be able to feel a pea underneath twenty mattresses!'

The queen went to a spare bedroom. She placed a tiny pea on the bed and called for her maidservants to search all over the castle and collect all the bedding they could find. They searched in every room of the castle. The maidservants found twenty mattresses and laid them one on top of the other on the bed and then twenty eiderdowns were put on top of the mattresses. The mattresses and the eiderdowns were all kinds of different colours and patterns.

When they had finally finished, the queen called the young girl and told her they had made a comfortable bed where she could sleep for the night.

The princess came to the bedroom, where the queen showed her the bed that they had prepared for her, and where she was to sleep for the night. It was so high up that the queen's maidservants had to go and fetch a tall ladder. The girl climbed right to the very top of the ladder and got into bed. The queen and her maidservants turned down the lights and left the young girl to sleep for the night. The princess lay down and tried to get to sleep, but she found it impossible. She tried lying on her left side, then on her right side, then on her back. She tried stretching out and curling up. But no matter what she tried, she simply could not get comfortable enough to fall asleep.

The following morning, all the members of the royal family went to the young girl's room to see how well she had slept.

'I hope you had a restful night and were comfortable', said the queen. 'I am so very sorry', the girl replied. 'I really do not want to appear ungrateful, but I am afraid I simply could not get a wink of sleep at all! I barely managed to close my eyes all night'.

'Heaven only knows what was in that bed, but I was lying on something so large and so hard that it felt as if there was a boulder underneath me. I am bruised black and blue all over my body. It was truly terrible!'

Much to the young girl's surprise, the queen seemed to be completely delighted by this news.

'I am so very happy my dear', the queen explained, 'for you see, this proves that you are truly a real princess. I know that nobody but a genuine princess could possibly have skin so sensitive that she could feel a tiny pea underneath twenty mattresses and twenty eiderdowns!'

The princess immediately understood and was very happy. So, of course, was the king, and especially the young prince. He had travelled far and wide to find a real princess and just as he had been starting to believe that he would never succeed, one had arrived right at his door!

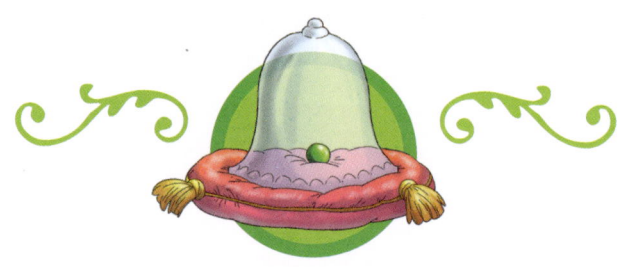

Luckily, it was soon discovered that the princess had fallen just as much in love with the prince as he was with her. Soon afterwards, they were married and there was great rejoicing and celebrations throughout the kingdom.
In time, they had many children. The prince duly became king and the princess became his queen, and they lived a full and happy life.

And what became of the pea? Well, it was placed underneath a crystal cloche and put in a special place in the castle museum, where it may still be found to this very day! And that is a true story!

The End

Thumbelina

Once upon a time there lived a woman. She wanted very much to have a little child, but she could not get her wish to come true. Eventually she went to a fairy, and said: 'I should like so very much to have a little child. Can you help me please and tell me where I can find one?' 'Oh, that can be very easily managed', said the fairy. 'Here is a barleycorn that is different to the sort that grows in the farmer's fields, and which the chickens eat. Take it back to your home, plant it in a flower pot and see what happens'.

'Thank you', said the woman, and she gave the fairy twelve shillings, which was just the price of the barleycorn.

The woman returned home and planted the corn. Immediately, up grew up a large and handsome flower. It was something like a tulip, but with its leaves tightly closed as if it were still a bud. 'It is a beautiful flower,' said the woman. Within the flower, upon the green velvet stamens, sat a very delicate and graceful little maiden. She was scarcely half as long as a thumb and the woman named her Thumbelina, because she was so small.

Her bed was made from a walnut shell filled with violet leaves and with a rose leaf for a counterpane. Here she slept at night, but during the day she sang. Thumbelina could sing so softly and sweetly that nothing like her singing had ever been heard before.

One night while everyone was asleep, a large, ugly wet toad crept in through a broken pane of glass in the window. 'What a pretty little wife this girl would make for my son', said the toad, and she picked up the walnut shell with Thumbelina inside and jumped through the window into the garden, where she placed it on one of the water lily leaves out in the stream. Thumbelina woke very early the next morning, and when she found out where she was, she began to weep.

The old toad said to her: 'Here is my son, he will be your husband, and you will live happily in the marsh by the stream'. 'Croak, croak', said the ugly son. Thumbelina could not bear to think of living with such a creature.

Soon, little fish gnawed the leaf loose with their teeth, so it floated down the stream. Then a butterfly saw Thumbelina. With her girdle tied round the butterfly, they flew far away.
Presently a large May bug flew by. The moment he caught sight of Thumbelina, he wrapped his claws round her delicate waist and flew off with her into a tree. After a while all the other May bugs turned up their feelers and said, 'She only has two legs! How ugly that looks!' 'Her waist is slim. Pooh! She is ugly', said another. The May bug believed all the others, so he took her down to the ground, placed her on a daisy and flew away. And all the while she was really the loveliest creature that anyone could imagine.

Thumbelina lived alone during the summer. But soon the summer passed, together with the birds who sang for her, and then came autumn and then winter – the long, cold winter. She wandered around because her house was not built against the cold.

She came at last to the door of a field mouse, who had a little den under the corn stubble. The mouse lived in warmth and comfort, with a whole roomful of corn, a kitchen and a beautiful dining room. 'You poor little creature', said the field mouse, 'come into my warm room and dine with me'. 'You are quite welcome to stay with me all the winter if you like, but you must keep my rooms clean and neat and tell me stories'.

One day, the mouse's neighbour, the mole, came to visit and saw Thumbelina. He was rich and learned, no doubt, but he spoke belittlingly of the sun and the pretty flowers because he had never seen them. The mouse suggested Thumbelina should take the mole as her husband, so she could be well provided for. 'But he is blind', said the mouse, 'so you must tell him a lot of your pretty stories'. Thumbelina was not at all interested in the mole, for he did not like the sun. Thumbelina was obliged to sing to him, 'Ladybird, ladybird, fly away home', and many other pretty songs. And the mole fell in love with her, because she had such a sweet voice.

The mole took Thumbelina out for long walks in the tunnels that he had dug under the ground. One day during their walk, they came across a bird lying on the ground. It was a perfect and beautiful swallow, with its beak and feathers intact, and could not have been dead for long. The mole did not care about the bird and walked on. 'Farewell, pretty little bird', said Thumbelina and she laid her head on the bird's chest. 'Thump, thump', she heard.

What she could hear was the bird's heart, for he was not really dead at all. Thumbelina put her warm woollen scarf over the poor swallow and during the night she came back to hide the bird in a safe place.

The next morning she stole out to see the bird. He was alive but very weak and could only open his eyes for a moment to look at Thumbelina. 'Thank you, pretty little maiden', said the sick swallow. 'I have been so nicely warmed, that I shall soon regain my strength and be able to fly about again in the warm sunshine'.

'Oh', said Thumbelina, 'it is cold outside now; there is snow and frost. Stay in your warm bed and I will take care of you'. The swallow remained underground for the whole winter and Thumbelina nursed him with love and care. Neither the mole nor the field mouse knew anything about it, for they did not like swallows.

One morning the mouse called Thumbelina. 'You are going to be wed, tiny girl', he said. 'My neighbour has asked for your hand in marriage. What good fortune for a poor child like you. Now we must prepare your wedding clothes'. The field mouse hired four spiders, who were to weave day and night to make the wedding dress. Thumbelina was not at all pleased, for she did not really like the tiresome mole, but the mouse did not want to listen to what she was saying. 'Nonsense', he said. 'He is a very handsome mole indeed and the queen herself does not wear more beautiful velvets and furs'.

When the autumn arrived, Thumbelina had her outfit made for her and was quite ready.

So the day was fixed for the wedding, when the mole would fetch Thumbelina to live with him deep under the earth. Never again would Thumbelina see the warm sun, because the mole did not like it. 'Farewell bright sun', she cried, stretching out her arms towards it when she walked outside in her wedding dress. Suddenly came the sound 'tweet, tweet' from above her. She looked up, and there was the swallow flying close by. 'Take me with you!' called Thumbelina. The swallow picked her up from the ground, she seated herself on the bird's back and they flew away, leaving the mole behind with no wife.

They arrived on a tree, in a sunny field full of flowers. 'This is my house', said the swallow, 'but it would not do for you to live here. You would not be comfortable. You must choose one of those flowers. I will put you down upon it and then you shall have everything you need to make you happy'. So she picked a beautiful white flower. In it stood a handsome little prince. When he saw Thumbelina, the prince was delighted. He thought she was the prettiest little maiden he had ever seen. So he took his golden crown from his head, and placed it on hers. They fell in love and were married. She received a pair of wings from the king and queen to accompany her husband on his travels from flower to flower, and a new name: Maia.

The End

The Little Mermaid

Far out in the deep ocean, there was a magical underwater kingdom. Its ruler was the sea king, who lived in a magnificent castle. His wife had passed away and he was left with six daughters. The sea princesses had no feet, but their bodies ended in a fish's tail. The youngest was the prettiest of them all. Her eyes were as blue as the deepest sea and her skin was as smooth and delicate as a rose petal. She was quiet and thoughtful. Unlike her sisters, who delighted in wonderful things, she cared for nothing but the beautiful flowers growing in the garden surrounding the castle.

On their fifteenth birthday, each princess was allowed to swim to the surface to look at the world above. Each of the little mermaid's sisters returned with amazing stories and she listened longingly to their various descriptions of the surface and of human beings. She made her grandmother tell her all she knew about the ships and the town, the people and the animals. The old mermaid said: 'When you reach fifteen, you will have permission to rise up out of the sea and sit on the rocks in the moonlight, while the great ships sail by'.

The day came and the sun had just set as the little mermaid raised her head above the waves. A large ship was in sight and there was music and song on board. The little mermaid swam closer. There were sailors on deck and among them was a young prince. He was the most beautiful of them all, with large black eyes. The prince was at the helm and he looked captivating. The little mermaid could not take her eyes off the ship or the handsome prince.

Then heavy clouds darkened the sky and the sea became restless. Lightning appeared in the distance and the waves rose high. The little mermaid saw they were in danger.

The ship groaned and creaked. Before long, the thick planks of the deck started to break under the weight of the sea and water rushed into the ship. All swam for their lives. The little mermaid remembered that human beings could not live under the water, but she could not see the young prince. She swam between the beams and planks that floated around but she could not find him. Then she dived deep under the water where she managed to reach the prince. His eyes were closed and his limbs did not move. She held his head above the water and dragged him to the shore.

The prince did not know that the little mermaid had saved his life and she returned to her father's castle feeling very sad. She feared the prince would marry someone else and she would die. Her grandmother explained: 'Humans have a much shorter life than merfolk's three hundred years. When mermaids die they turn to sea foam, while humans have an eternal soul that lives on in Heaven'. 'And your fish's tail, which among us is considered so beautiful, is thought on earth to be quite ugly', her grandmother continued. The little mermaid sighed and looked sorrowfully at her tail. 'Is there anything I can do to win his heart?'

Longing for human legs so that she could return to the surface and meet the handsome prince, the little mermaid went to the sea witch. 'I will give you legs and a human soul', screeched the old witch. 'But with every step you take, you will feel a pain as if you were walking on swords. And remember', continued the witch, 'you can never return to the sea or to your father's castle. And if you do not win the love of the prince and he does not marry you, you will die'. The little mermaid agreed to the witch's proposal. 'And in return', the witch said, 'I will take your sweet voice.'

The witch gave the little mermaid a bottle containing a potion, telling her that she must drink it when she reached the shore. The little mermaid left her underwater home and swam as fast as she could until she reached the beach near to the prince's palace. Holding the potion the sea witch had given to her, she opened the bottle and drank all of it. Almost straight away, it felt as if a sword had cut her beautiful tail in two and she fainted in pain. When she woke up, the very first thing she saw was the beautiful prince's eyes, but she could not speak a word.

The prince took the little mermaid to his grand palace. 'What is your name?' he asked, but the little mermaid had given her voice to the old sea witch, so she was unable to answer him. The prince dressed her in the most beautiful robes of the finest silk. Each day, servants at the castle would sing for the royal family and some sang better than others. The prince clapped his hands and smiled at the songs, but the little mermaid knew that her singing had once been much more beautiful. 'If only the prince could know my sweet singing!' she thought, 'but I gave away my voice forever simply to be with him'.

The young prince took good care of the little mermaid, but she could say nothing, and he did not realise that she was in love with him.

Then one day, the king and queen declared to all that the time had come for the young prince to be married. The youngest princess of the neighbouring country was suitable, and would become his bride. Learning of this news, the little mermaid became very sad. She remembered what the old sea witch had told her, and knew that if the prince were to marry anyone but her, she would die the next morning. 'And then I would never ever be able to see him again', she sighed.

Thinking of nothing other than the prince, and of what was to become of her, the little mermaid wandered back to the beach, where she sat alone, crying.

All of a sudden, her sisters appeared from beneath the waves. They had missed her so much that they too had been to visit the old sea witch. In exchange for their beautiful hair, the witch had given them a magical knife. 'If you kill the prince with this knife, you can come back with us and live as a mermaid again!' one of them said. 'We all miss you so very much and we want you to return home.'

But the little mermaid loved the prince too much and threw away the knife. The young prince came running, looking for her. When he found her, he took her head in his hands. Looking into her tearful eyes, he suddenly recognised her. 'You are the girl that saved my life! I have been looking for you everywhere. It is you!' he whispered softly to her. He fell in love with her forever and they were married. On the wedding day, her sisters came to watch the wonderful event. And as the little mermaid had captured the heart of a human man, she regained her sweet voice. In the warm evenings she would sing to the prince, and they lived happily ever after.

The End

The Emperor's New Clothes

Many years ago lived an emperor. Although he was a kind man, he was exceedingly vain and was so fond of new clothes that he spent all his money on them in order to be always beautifully dressed.

He did not care about his ministers; he did not care about the theatre. In truth, he only really liked to look at himself in the mirror, or to go out walking in order to show off his newest clothes. He had a different coat for every hour of every day and just like people usually say of a king, 'He is in the council chamber', here, the people always said, 'The emperor is in the wardrobe!'

In the great city in which the emperor lived, there was always something going on and there was soon to be a  great procession, which would be led by the emperor himself. Every day many strangers came to the city and one day two imposters arrived there. They announced themselves to be great weavers and said that they knew how to manufacture the most beautiful fabric ever imaginable.

Not only were the textures and patterns of this fabric uncommonly beautiful, but the clothes which were made out of the material possessed a wonderful property. They were completely invisible to anyone who was not fit for office, or who was unpardonably stupid!

'Those must indeed be the most splendid clothes', thought the emperor. 'If I were to wear them, I could find out who in my kingdom is unfit for the office they hold. I could distinguish the wise from the stupid! Yes, this fabric must be woven for me at once'. And he gave the two weavers a great deal of money, so that they might begin their work straight away.

The imposters put together two weaving looms, and began to act as if they were working, but they had not the slightest thing on the looms. They also demanded the finest silk and the best gold, which they placed in their pockets, and they worked at the empty looms late into the night.

'I should like to know how far they have got with the clothes', thought the emperor. But he remembered that anyone who was stupid or not fit for office would not be able to see the fabric. He certainly believed he had nothing to fear, but he wanted to send somebody else first in order to see how he stood with regard to his office. Everybody in the whole city knew what wonderful powers the fabric possessed, and they were all curious to see how bad or how stupid their neighbour was. 'I will send my old and honoured minister to the weavers', thought the emperor. 'He can judge what the fabric is like, for he has intellect and nobody knows their office better than he'.

So the minister went to where the weavers sat working at the empty looms. 'I can see nothing!' he thought, but he did not say so. The imposters asked him, 'Is the texture not beautiful and are the colours not lovely?' They pointed to the looms and the poor old minister looked, yet he could see nothing, for there was nothing there! 'Can I be stupid?' he thought. 'If so, nobody must know! Can I be not fit for office? No! I must not say that I cannot see the cloth!' 'Have you nothing to say about it?' asked one of the imposters. 'It is most lovely!' answered the minister. 'What texture! What colours! I will tell the emperor it pleases me greatly'.

The imposters now wanted more money, more silk and more gold. They put it all in their pockets and carried on as they had before, working at the empty looms. The emperor soon sent another statesman to see how the weaving was getting on and whether the clothes would soon be ready. Just as the minister before, he looked and looked, but could see nothing. 'Is it not beautiful cloth?' asked the two weavers, pointing to the empty looms. 'I am not stupid!' thought the man. 'It must be my good office for which I am not fit. It is strange, but no one must be allowed to know'. And so he praised the cloth and expressed his delight at the beautiful colours and the splendid texture.

By now, everybody was talking about the magnificent cloth and the emperor wanted to see it too, so he went to the weavers.

'Is it not splendid, your Majesty?' said the statesmen who had already been. 'What texture! What colours!' they declared, pointing at the empty loom.

'I can see nothing!' thought the emperor. 'This is terrible! Am I stupid? This cannot be.' 'It is indeed beautiful', he said. He nodded with gracious approval, for he could not say that he could see nothing. The whole court round him nodded too. 'Splendid! Lovely!' everyone shouted. They all seemed delighted and the imposters were given the title of Court Weavers to the Emperor.

The whole night before the procession, the imposters worked by candle light. People could see they were busy making the emperor's new clothes. They pretended to take the cloth from the loom, cut with scissors in the air, sewed with needles without thread, and said at last: 'The clothes are ready!'

The emperor came with his most distinguished knights and each weaver held up an arm as if holding something, and said: 'See! Here are the breeches! Here the coat!' and so on. 'Spun clothes are so comfortable, one would imagine one had nothing on at all!' 'Yes', said the knights, but they could see nothing, for there was nothing there!

'Will it please your Majesty to take off your clothes', said the imposters, 'then we will dress you in the new ones'. So the emperor did and the imposters stood before him as if they were putting on each item of the new clothes. Finally, the emperor turned and bent in front of the mirror. 'How beautifully they fit! said everybody. 'What material! What colours! It is truly a gorgeous suit!'

'They are waiting outside with the canopy which your Majesty is wont to have borne over you in the procession', announced the master of ceremonies.

'Look! I am ready', said the emperor. 'Does it not sit well?' And he turned again to the mirror to see that his finery was on right.

The chamberlains, who were used to carrying the train, put their hands near the floor as if they were lifting it, then they acted as if they were holding something in the air. Just as all the others, they did not want anyone to think that they could see absolutely nothing there.

So the procession got underway and the emperor walked along under the splendid canopy. Wherever they passed, all the people in the streets and at their doors and windows called out: 'Look how matchless are the emperor's new clothes! That wonderful train fastened to his suit, how beautifully it hangs!'

No one wanted the others to think they could see nothing, for then they would have been unfit for office, or else very stupid. Suddenly, in a quiet moment a little boy's voice was heard: 'The emperor isn't wearing any clothes!' he said. In that moment, the crowd began to realise it was true and people started to whisper. 'He has nothing on!' called out the people at last and they laughed.

This struck the emperor, for he realised they were right, but he thought to himself, 'I must go on with the procession'. And the chamberlains walked along still more upright, holding up the train which was not there at all!

The End

The Steadfast Tin Soldier

Once upon a time there were twenty-five tin soldiers, all brothers. Their uniforms were red and blue, and they shouldered their guns and looked straight ahead. The first words that they ever heard, when the lid of the box in which they lay was taken off, were: 'Hurrah, tin soldiers!' This was joyously exclaimed by a little boy, clapping his hands. They had been given to him because it was his birthday, and he began setting them out on the table. Each was exactly the same, except just one, who had been made last when the tin had run short. There he stood, as firmly on his one leg as the others did on two, and he is the one that became famous.

There were many other playthings on the table, but the nicest was a little cardboard castle, with windows through which you could see into the rooms. In front stood some little trees surrounding a mirror, like a lake. That was all very pretty, but the most beautiful thing was a little lady made of paper, who stood in the open doorway. She had a dress of the finest muslin and a scarf of blue ribbon fastened with a glittering rose, made of gold paper as big as her head. The little lady was stretching out her arms, for she was a dancer, and was lifting one leg up so high that the tin soldier couldn't see it and thought that she too had only one leg.

He hid behind a box, from where he could watch the lady. When night came, the children went to bed and the toys began to play! The nutcrackers played leapfrog and the pencil ran round the slate. There was such noise that the canary began to sing! The only two who never stirred were the tin soldier and the little dancer. She stayed on tiptoe; he stood steadfastly on his one leg, never taking his eyes from her. The clock struck twelve. Crack! Off flew the box lid and out popped a little imp. 'Don't look at things that aren't meant for the likes of you!' said the imp, but the soldier took no notice. 'Very well. Wait until tomorrow!'

When it was morning and the children had got up, the tin soldier was put by the window. Whether it was the wind or the little imp, all at once the window flew open and out fell the little tin soldier, head over heels! What a terrible fall! He landed on his head with his one leg in the air and his gun wedged between two paving stones.

The nursery maid and the little boy went down at once to look for him, but though they were so near him that they almost trod on him, they did not notice him. If the tin soldier had only called out: 'Here I am!' they would have found him, but he did not think it fitting for him to cry out, because he was wearing his uniform.

Soon it began to drizzle, then the drops came faster and before long there was a real downpour. When it was over, two street boys came along. 'Look!' cried one. 'A tin soldier! He shall sail in a boat!'

So the boys made a little boat out of newspaper, put the tin soldier in it and sailed it up and down the gutter. The boys ran alongside, clapping their hands. What great big waves there were and what a swift current! The little boat tossed up and down and it went so quickly that the soldier trembled, but he remained steadfast. All at once the boat passed into a long tunnel that was as dark as his box had been.

'Where can I be going now?' he wondered. 'Oh, dear me! I'm absolutely certain this is all the imp's fault! Ah, if only the little lady were sitting beside me in the boat, it could be twice as dark for all I should care!'

All of a sudden, along came a great big water rat who lived in the tunnel. 'Have you got your passport?' asked the rat. 'Out with your passport! Quickly!' But the tin soldier remained silent and steadfast, and grasped his gun more firmly.

The boat sped on with the rat running behind it. He cried out to the floating bits of wood and straw: 'Hold on to him! Hold on to him! He has not yet paid the toll! He has not yet shown his passport!'

But the current became swifter and stronger. The tin soldier could already see daylight where the tunnel ended, but to his ears there came a roaring sound, loud enough to frighten any brave man. Just think! If at the end of the tunnel the gutter flowed into a great canal, it would be as dangerous for him as it would be for us to go down a waterfall! Now he was so near to it that he could not hold on any longer. On went the boat, the poor tin soldier keeping himself as stiff as he could, for no one should say of him afterwards that he had flinched. The boat whirled round three, four times, and became full to the brim with water. It began to sink!

The tin soldier stood up to his neck in water. The boat sank deeper and the paper grew softer, until the water was nearly over the soldier's head. But all he could think of was the pretty little dancer, whose face he would never see again. Finally, the paper came apart and the soldier fell into the water, but at the last moment he was swallowed by a great big fish. How dark it was inside the fish! Even darker than in the tunnel and it was really very close quarters! But there lay the steadfast tin soldier full length, still shouldering his gun. Up and down swam the fish, then without warning it made the most dreadful contortions and became suddenly quite still.

Then it was as if a flash of lightning had passed through him. Daylight streamed in and a voice exclaimed, 'Why, here is the little tin soldier!' The fish had been caught, taken to market, sold and brought into the kitchen. There, the cook had cut it open with a great knife. She picked up the soldier and carried him into the room, where everyone wanted to see the hero who had been found inside a fish, but the tin soldier was not at all proud. They put him on the table, but what strange things do happen in this world! The tin soldier was in the same room in which he had been before! He saw the same children and the same toys on the table. And there was the same pretty castle with the beautiful little dancer.

The little dancer was still there, standing on one leg with the other high in the air, as she too was steadfast. That touched the tin soldier and he was almost going to shed some tin tears, but that would not have been fitting for a soldier. He looked at her, but she said nothing. The maid put the soldier on the table where the young boy found him. Now, he was not the horrible sort of boy who would throw the soldier into the fire, but his little sister opened the jack-in-the-box and the imp jumped out and tickled the boy's ear. He was so shocked, that in his surprise he dropped the tin soldier into the fire. The imp just looked on, smiling an evil smile.

Just at that very moment, the maid came into the room. The draught of the door opening caught up the beautiful little dancer and off she flew like a tiny sylph, straight into the fire next to the tin soldier. She burst into flames, and that was the end of her! In the heat of the fire, the poor tin soldier melted down into a little lump. The next morning, when the maid was taking out the ashes of the fire, she found that the steadfast little tin soldier had turned into the shape of a tiny, tin heart. There was nothing to be found of the little dancer but her golden rose, right beside the tin heart and burned as black as a cinder.

The End

The Wild Swans

*I*n a faraway kingdom, there once lived a king with his twelve children: eleven princes and one princess. One day he decided to remarry, but without knowing beforehand, he married a wicked queen who was actually a witch and who did not love the poor children at all. They knew this from the very first day after the wedding, because in the palace, instead of cakes and apples she gave them some sand in a teacup and told them to pretend it was cake.

The week after that, she sent the princess, little Elisa, into the country to live with a peasant and his wife. Then she told the king so many untrue things about the young princes, that he no longer had any respect for them.

Out of spite, the queen lured the princes away from the castle. She turned her eleven stepsons into swans and forced them to fly away. 'Go out into the world and get your own living,' said the queen. 'Fly like great birds, who have no voice'.

They twisted their long necks and flapped their wings, but no one heard them so they had to fly away. But the queen could not make them ugly, as she had wished, for they had been turned into eleven, beautiful wild swans. Then, with a strange cry, they flew past the windows of the palace, over the park and on to the forest beyond. Years went by and Elisa returned home.

The queen became ever more jealous of Elisa, as people told her the girl was as beautiful as a perfect rose. One morning the queen went into the bathroom and filled the bath. Taking some toads, she kissed them, put them into the water and said to them, 'When Elisa gets into the bath, seat yourselves on her head so that she may become as stupid and ugly as you are, and make her heart evil'. She then called Elisa, and helped her into the bath. But the spell did not work. The frogs changed into red roses, because Elisa's goodness was too strong. Seeing this, the queen was so angry that she made Elisa unrecognisable with walnut juice and banished her to a dark forest.

The poor girl had also to take a vow of silence, for the witch told her that speaking one word would kill her brothers. Elisa wept and thought of her brothers, far away. She kept on walking through the deep forest. Days went by and finally she reached the ocean. Just as the sun was about to set, Elisa saw eleven white swans with golden crowns on their heads, flying towards her, one behind the other like a long white ribbon. Elisa hid in the bushes. The swans landed quite close to her and flapped their great white wings. As soon as the sun had disappeared behind the sea, the feathers of the swans dropped off and eleven handsome princes stood near her.

Elisa recognised them immediately and rushed into their arms with great happiness. They all laughed with joy. 'We brothers', said the eldest, 'fly about as wild swans so long as the sun is in the sky, but as soon as it sinks behind the hills, we return to our human shape. Therefore we must always be near a resting place for our feet before sunset'. 'How can I break this spell?' said their sister. But no one could answer this question. 'Tomorrow', said one, 'we shall fly away, not to return again until a whole year has passed. Will you come with us Elisa?' 'Yes, take me with you', said the princess, so during the night they made a net to carry her over the ocean.

Elisa laid down in the net, and when the sun rose and her brothers became wild swans again, they picked up the net with their beaks and flew up to the clouds. Each night they had to rest on rocks until they changed back again into swans by day. Each day they flew onward through the air like a winged arrow. As the sun rose higher one day, Elisa fell into a deep sleep. She dreamt of a fairy. 'Your brothers can be released', she said, 'if you only have courage and perseverance. You must spin and weave eleven coats with the stinging nettles that grow round the graves in a churchyard. Only these can be used'.

After the long journey, they finally arrived in a new land and Elisa went straight to begin her work. She found the ugly nettles. They burned blisters on her hands and arms, but she determined to bear it gladly in order to free her brothers. She kept at her work day and night. One coat was already finished and she had begun the second, when she heard a huntsman's horn in the early morning. The sound came nearer and nearer and she heard dogs barking. Suddenly a handsome man stood in front of her. It was the king of the county. 'How did you come here, my sweet child?' he asked. Elisa could not speak or her brothers would die. 'Come with me', he said. The king had never seen a more beautiful girl.

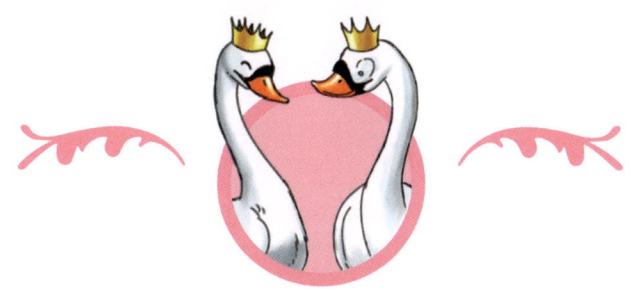

He gave Elisa beautiful new clothes. The handsome king immediately fell in love with her and he proposed to crown her as his queen and wife. She agreed, but the archbishop was jealous. He shook his head and whispered that the fair young maiden was nothing other than a witch, who had blinded the king's eyes and bewitched his heart. The king would hear nothing of this. At night Elisa crept away into her little chamber and quickly wove one coat after another. She had almost finished her task. Only one coat remained to be completed, but she found that she had no more nettles.

Leaving the castle in silence, she crept through the garden in the broad moonlight and passed through the narrow alleys and deserted streets, until finally she reached the churchyard. Here, she came across a terrible group of ghouls and demons. Elisa had to pass close by them, but they did not hurt her and so she picked the burning nettles and carried them back home to the castle. But one person had seen her: the archbishop. He was awake while everybody else was asleep. The next day he told the king what he had seen and insisted that Elisa must be a witch. 'She has bewitched you and all the people', said the archbishop.

This time the king believed the archbishop and put Elisa on trial for witchcraft. She could speak no words in her defence, and was sentenced to death by burning at the stake. She was thrown into a dreary cell with her coats and a bundle of nettles. She kept on knitting, because one coat was still unfinished. The sun rose and all the people came to see the witch burned. They placed her on a pile of wood, but at the same moment, eleven wild swans flew over her and alighted on the ground.

She hastily threw the eleven coats over the swans and they immediately turned back into handsome princes, but a sleeve of one coat was unfinished, so one brother kept a wing instead of an arm. 'Now I can speak', she exclaimed. 'I am innocent!'

The people, who had seen what happened, bowed to her. 'Yes, she is innocent', said the eldest brother. Immediately, all the pieces of wood where she was standing turned into roses. The king plucked one flower and gave it to Elisa. The next day the church bells rang and birds came in great flocks. And a marriage feast was held in the castle, such as no king had ever before seen.

And they lived happily ever after.

The End

The Nightingale

Many years ago in China there lived an emperor. The emperor was a Chinaman, as were all those around him. The emperor's palace was the most beautiful in the world. It was built entirely out of porcelain and was very costly, but so delicate and fragile that whoever touched it was obliged to be careful. In the garden could be seen the most amazing flowers, with pretty silver bells tied to them. The bells tinkled so that everyone who passed could not help noticing the flowers. Indeed, everything in the emperor's garden was remarkable and it extended so far that the gardener himself did not know where it ended.

Those who travelled beyond the garden's limits knew that there was a noble forest, with lofty trees. The forest sloped down to the deep blue sea and great ships sailed under the shadows of the trees. In one of these tall trees lived a nightingale. The little bird sang so beautifully that even the poor fishermen, who had so many other things to do, would stop and listen. Sometimes, when they sailed at night to spread their nets, they would hear the nightingale sing, and would say, 'Oh, is that not beautiful?' But when they returned from their fishing, they forgot about the bird until the next night. Then they would hear her again, and exclaim 'Oh, how beautiful is the nightingale's song!'

Travellers from around the world came to the city. They admired the palace and gardens, but when they heard the nightingale they declared it to be the best of all. And on their return home, they wrote books including the palace, the gardens and the greatest wonder of all, the nightingale. These books were sent everywhere and came into the hands of the emperor. He sat in his golden chair and as he read, he nodded in approval. It pleased him to find such beautiful descriptions of his palace and gardens, but when he came to the words, 'the nightingale is the most beautiful of all,' he was surprised. 'I know nothing of a nightingale', he said. 'Is there such a bird in my empire? And even in my garden? I have never heard it'.

'I will hear the nightingale. She must be here this evening', said the emperor. 'She has my highest favour and if she does not come, the whole court shall be trampled upon after supper is ended'. His lord in waiting was ordered to find the nightingale. He ran up and down stairs, through all the halls and corridors and half the court ran with him. Finally he found a poor little girl in the kitchen who knew the nightingale quite well. She was offered a good job, 'If you will lead us to the nightingale, for she is invited for this evening to the palace'. So the girl went to the wood where the nightingale sang, and half the court followed.

'Hark, hark! There she is', said the little girl, 'and there she sits', she added, pointing to a little grey bird who was perched on a branch high up in a tree. 'Is this possible?' said the lord in waiting, 'I never imagined the nightingale would be such a little, plain and simple looking thing as that. She has certainly changed colour at seeing so many grand people around her!' 'Little nightingale', cried the girl, raising her voice, 'our most gracious emperor wishes for you to sing before him'. 'With the greatest pleasure', said the nightingale, and began to sing most delightfully. 'Little nightingale', said a courtier, 'I have the great honour of inviting you to the court festival at the emperor's palace this evening'.

The palace was elegantly decorated for the occasion. In the centre of the great hall, a golden perch had been placed for the nightingale. When the bird began to sing, tears came into the emperor's eyes, and then rolled down his cheeks, as her song became still more beautiful and touched everyone's hearts. The emperor was so delighted that he offered his gold slipper to wear round her neck, but she declined the honour gracefully. 'I have seen tears in an emperor's eyes', the nightingale said. 'That is my richest reward. An emperor's tears have wonderful power and are quite sufficient honour for me'. And then she sang again, more enchantingly than ever.

The whole city spoke of the wonderful bird and nothing else was talked of. One day the emperor received a large package on which was written 'The Nightingale'. It was a work of art contained in a beautiful wooden casket. An artificial nightingale made to look like a living one, and covered completely in diamonds, rubies and sapphires. Once it had been wound up, it could sing like the real one and move its tail up and down. It was the nightingale that belonged to the emperor of Japan, but it was poor compared with that of the emperor of China. 'Now they must sing together', said the court, 'and what a duet that will be'.

But they did not get on well, for the real nightingale sang in its own, natural way and the artificial bird sang only waltzes. The artificial bird was as successful as the real one, besides, it was so much prettier to look at, for it sparkled like the finest jewellery. So it sang the same tunes thirty-three times, but where was the living nightingale when the emperor called for her? No one had noticed her when she flew out of the open window, back to her own green woods. All the courtiers blamed her for being a very ungrateful creature and the artificial bird was placed on a silk cushion by the emperor's bed.

Another year passed, and the emperor, the court, and all the other people knew every little note of the artificial bird's song, and for that same reason it pleased them better. They could sing with the bird, which they often did. One evening when the artificial bird was singing its best and the emperor lay in bed listening to it, something inside the bird sounded 'whizz'. Then a spring cracked. 'Whir-r-r-r' went all the wheels, turning round, and the music stopped. The emperor immediately sprang out of bed and called for a watchmaker to fix the bird. But it was impossible to repair without spoiling the music. Five years passed and then great grief came upon the land. The emperor became very ill.

Cold and pale lay the emperor in his royal bed. A window stood open and the moon shone in upon the emperor and the artificial bird. 'Sing! Sing' shouted the emperor. 'You little precious golden bird, sing, pray sing! I have given you gold and costly presents. Sing!' But the bird remained silent. There was no one to wind it up. Suddenly, there came through the open window the sound of sweet music. Outside, on the branch of a tree, sat the living nightingale. She had heard of the emperor's illness and had come to sing to him of hope and trust. And as she sang, the shadows grew paler and paler. The blood in the emperor's veins flowed more rapidly and brought life to his weak limbs.

The emperor became strong again. 'Thank you, thank you, you heavenly little bird. I know you well. I banished you from my kingdom once with your sweet song. How can I reward you?' 'You have already rewarded me', said the nightingale. 'I shall never forget that I drew tears from your eyes the first time I sang to you. These are the jewels that rejoice a singer's heart. But now sleep and grow strong and well again. I will sing to you again, so that you may be happy, but let nobody know that you have a little bird who tells you everything. It will be best to conceal it'. So saying, the nightingale flew away.

And a great festival was organised for the emperor who was alive and healthy once more.

The End

The Ugly Duckling

It was a golden afternoon in late summer. Near a big old farm in the country, a mother duck had made a nest by the water. 'These eggs are taking a long time to hatch', she sighed. She was lonely sitting there all by herself. The other ducks were too busy swimming around to come and chat to her. At last the ducklings began to peck their way out of the eggs. Their little beaks banged away against the shell. One by one, still wet from the egg, they tumbled onto the floor of the nest. Soon, they stood up and shook themselves until their soft downy feathers became dry and fluffy. The little ducklings stared with wonder. 'How big the world is!' they chirped.

'Oh, the world is much bigger than this', quacked the mother duck. 'Now, is everyone hatched? Oh dear, no! That one big egg is still there!'

An old duck swam by and stopped to look. 'Look at the size of that! It must be a turkey egg', she said. 'I had one in my nest once. What a worry it was! The chick simply would not go near the water, no matter how much I tried to push it. Just leave it alone, that's my advice'.

And she slowly swam away.

'I think I will sit on it a little while longer', said the mother duck. 'As I have sat so long already, a few days will really not matter very much'.

Before long, the mother duck heard a tapping noise and soon a new chick toppled out of the egg. 'Chirp! Chirp!' it cried. The mother stared at it and exclaimed, 'It is very large and not like the others. I wonder if it really is a turkey. Well, we shall soon see'. The mother duck led her family down to the water. Splash! In went the first duckling. One by one they disappeared under the surface and bobbed up again like little balloons. Soon all of them, even the ugly duckling, were gliding over the water. 'Oh,' said the mother, 'that is not a turkey. Look how well he uses his legs and how upright he floats! He is my child and is not so ugly if you look at him properly'.

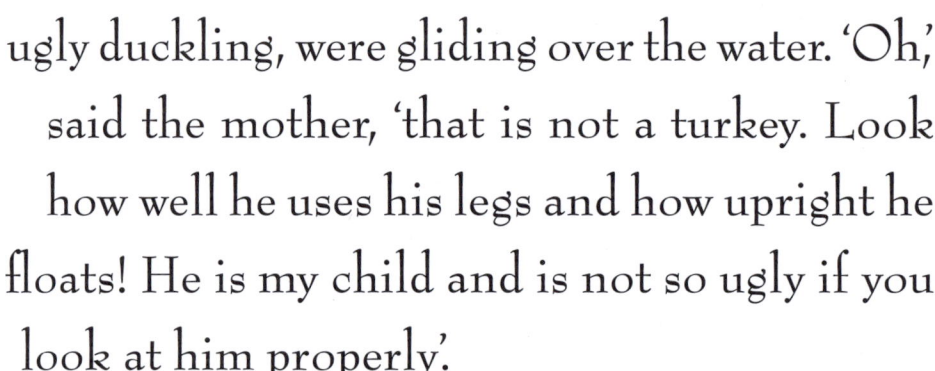

The next day, mother duck took her family to the barnyard. 'Pay your respects to the old duck', she said. The ducklings bowed, too much in awe to even chirp. Then the turkey marched up to look them over. 'I've never seen such a big, ugly duckling!' he gobbled. That was just the beginning of the duckling's troubles. Everyone was mean to him because he was so ugly. The ducks pecked him, the chickens beat him, and the girl who fed the poultry kicked him with her feet. The poor duckling was heartbroken, so at last he ran away, frightening the little birds in the hedge as he jumped over the fence.

He ran as fast as his big, webbed feet would go and soon he reached the woods. He found himself beside a great marsh where wild ducks lived. There he lay, hidden under a bush, feeling very lonely and tired.

In the morning, some wild ducks flew by and stopped to look at the new arrival. They looked very different from those in the barnyard. 'Who are you?' they asked. 'I'm a farm duck', said the ugly duckling. 'A duck?' they squawked. 'We've never seen a duckling like you! But we don't mind if you stay here a while, as the marsh is big enough for all of us'. The ugly duckling was glad to rest by the marsh, far away from the cruel animals on the farm.

Days later, two wild geese passed by. 'Hello!' they called. 'Would you like some company? Come along with us!' The ugly duckling was happy to, but before he could move, shots rang out. To his horror, the geese fell into the marsh and a huge dog splashed in to fetch them. Guns began firing all around the marsh. He turned his head to hide it under his wing and at that moment a big dog passed near him. He thrust his nose close to the duckling, showing his sharp teeth, but then, splash! He went into the water without touching the duckling. 'Thank goodness! I'm so ugly even the dogs don't want me', gasped the duckling. He lay there perfectly still, until the dogs disappeared and the firing stopped.

Then he ran and ran till a heavy storm came, but he managed to reach a little cottage. The duckling squeezed through a hole and huddled in a corner. An old woman lived in the cottage with a cat and hen, who were loved as if they were her children. The cat and the hen tried to reassure the duckling, 'Just lay eggs and learn to purr, and you'll be fine'. But he could do neither of these things, so for weeks he sat sadly in the corner, remembering the joy of gliding over the water. At last he said to the hen, 'I want to go into the wide world'. 'What an absurd idea,' said the hen. 'You have nothing else to do, therefore you have foolish ideas. If you could purr or lay eggs, they would go away, but I won't stop you'.

So the duckling left the cottage and soon found a big pond where he floated in the sun, day after day. Autumn came, and the leaves turned to orange and gold. One evening a large flock of beautiful birds arrived. The duckling had never seen anything like them before. They curved their graceful necks and their soft plumage was a dazzling white. They uttered an unusual cry, as they spread their glorious wings and flew away to warmer countries across the sea. As he watched them rise higher and higher into the air, the ugly little duckling felt a strange sensation. He stretched out his neck towards them, and uttered a cry so strange that he frightened himself.

Before long, the cold winter winds began to blow and the frost came. The duckling had to swim about on the water to keep it from freezing, but every night the space where he swam became smaller and smaller. At length it froze so hard that the ice in the water crackled as he moved and the duckling had to paddle with his legs as fast as he could, to keep the space from closing up. He became exhausted at last and lay still and helpless, frozen fast into the ice. Early in the morning, a peasant who was passing by saw what had happened. He broke the ice into pieces with his wooden shoe and carried the duckling home.

The warmth revived the poor little creature, but when the children went to play with him, the duckling was frightened. He started up in terror, fluttered into the milk pan and splashed milk all about the room. Then the children's mother clapped her hands, which frightened him still more. He flew into the butter cask, then into the meal tub and then out again. What a state he was in! The woman screamed and struck at him with tongs, the children laughed and tumbled over each other in their efforts to catch him, but luckily he escaped. The door stood open and he just managed to slip out among the bushes and lie down quite exhausted in the newly fallen snow.

The duckling survived the winter. When spring came, he stretched his wings. Before he knew it, he was flying towards a beautiful garden. In it was a big pond, where three beautiful birds were gliding gracefully over the water. They were swans, but he did not know it. 'I'll join them', he thought. 'Perhaps they'll kill me, but rather that than be pecked by hens'. He glided over to the swans and bowed his head. There, reflected in the water, was another swan! 'Look, there's a new one!' cried two children who had run into the garden. 'It's the prettiest of them all!' The swan, no longer an ugly duckling, lifted his graceful neck. His heart filled with love for the other swans and at last he had found true happiness.

The End

The Red Shoes

There once lived a little girl called Karen. She was very pretty, but so poor that she had to go barefoot all through the summer. In the winter she wore thick wooden shoes that chafed her ankles until they were as red as could be. Nearby lived the widow of an old shoemaker. The woman had some old scraps of red cloth and did her best to make them into a little pair of shoes. They were a bit clumsy, but well meant, for she intended to give them to the little girl to wear. The first time Karen wore her new red shoes was on the day when her mother was buried. Of course, they were not right for mourning, but they were all that she had.

Just then, a large old carriage came by, with an old lady inside it. She saw the poor little girl and took pity upon her. So the old lady went to see the parson and said, 'Give the little girl to me and I shall take good care of her'. Karen was sure this had happened because of her red shoes, but the old lady said that the shoes were horrible and ordered them to be burned. Karen was given proper new clothes and she was taught to read and to sew. People said that she was pretty, but her mirror told her, 'You are more than just pretty. You are beautiful!'

Some while later, the queen of the country came travelling with her little daughter, the young princess. Karen went along with all the other local people who flocked to see the royal family at the town's nearby castle. The little princess, dressed all in white, came out onto a balcony so that everyone could admire her. She did not wear a train and she did not wear a gold crown, but she did wear a pair of splendid, red leather shoes. Of course, they were much nicer than the ones that the old shoemaker's widow had made, but Karen thought to herself that there was still nothing in the world better than a pair of red shoes!

When Karen was old enough to be confirmed, new clothes were made for her and she was to have new shoes. They went to the town's best shoemaker so he could measure her feet. In his shop were big glass cases, filled with the prettiest shoes and the shiniest boots. Among them was a pair of red leather ones that were just like those the princess had worn. How perfect they were! As the shoes fitted Karen, the old lady bought them, but she had poor eyesight so had no idea they were red. If she had known, she would never have let Karen wear them to her confirmation, but that is just what Karen did!

On the day of her confirmation, everyone was looking at Karen's feet. When she walked up the aisle of the church, it seemed as if even the old paintings of bygone ministers and their wives, in starched ruffs and black gowns, were gazing at her red shoes. She could not concentrate during the service and could think of nothing other than her shoes! Before the day was over, the old lady had heard from almost everyone that the shoes were red. She told Karen it was really very naughty to wear red shoes to church and that in future she was always to wear black shoes, even though they were her old ones.

Next day Karen looked at her black shoes. She looked at her red ones. She kept looking at her red ones until she put them on. It was a fair, sunny day and Karen and the old lady took the path through the cornfield. In town they met an old soldier who noticed Karen's feet. 'Oh, what perfect shoes for dancing', the old soldier said. 'Never come off when you dance!' he told the shoes, and he tapped his sword on the sole of each one. And Karen could not help it, she felt obliged to dance a few steps and once she had begun, her legs continued to dance. It seemed as if the shoes had power over them, for she just could not stop!

At home later, the shoes were put into the cupboard but Karen could not help looking at them. That evening the old lady fell ill and could not leave her bed. She had to be cared for and given medicine. It was Karen's task to stay at home and do this, but there was a grand ball in the town, and she had been invited. She looked at the red shoes and put them on, thinking there was no harm in that. Then, ignoring her stepmother, she selfishly went to the ball. Once there, she started to dance, but when she wanted to go to the right, the shoes went to the left. When she wanted to dance up the room, the shoes danced down the room, down the stairs, through the street and right out through the gates of the town.

She was really frightened and wanted to throw the red shoes away, but she simply could not take them off! She tore off her stockings, but it was as if the shoes were stuck to her feet. She danced and  had to carry on dancing, over fields and meadows, through rain and sunshine, and right on into the dark of night — and by night it was the most horrible! No matter how much she wanted to, the red shoes just would not let her stop. After what seemed like ages, she eventually danced her way back to the ball, but by then it was too late. The ball had ended and everyone had gone home.

The shoes carried her far away, dancing over thorns and tree stumps. Eventually, she danced her way to a lonely little house. Inside, she saw the old soldier and she tapped with her finger on the window and said, 'Come out, come out! I cannot come in, for I must dance'. 'Well, well', replied the old soldier, 'look who is here!' 'Please take off my shoes', said Karen. 'They will not stop dancing and I need to go home to my stepmother to nurse her, or she will not get better. I'm really sorry for sneaking out to the ball instead of staying at home to help my stepmother'.

'Very good, Karen!' declared the old soldier. 'For the first time you are not thinking about yourself and are thinking about others. Remember this in future'. And saying this, he tapped with his sword against the tips of the red shoes.  Immediately they flew off, but instead of staying on the ground, the shoes kept on dancing and dancing. They danced away, across the field and into the deep forest beyond. Karen's poor little feet hurt and she could barely walk, but she thanked the old soldier for his kindness and hurried back to her home, where her ill stepmother was lying in bed.

When Karen eventually reached her home, she went straight up to her stepmother's bedroom. Falling into the arms of the old lady she started to cry sad and bitter tears and asked for forgiveness. Her stepmother saw the true remorse in Karen's eyes and immediately forgave her. From that day on, Karen carried out her tasks and nursed her stepmother, until in time, the old lady became well again. Karen had never been happier than she was then, and for the rest of her life, she never thought about wearing red shoes ever again!

The End

*I*t was New Year's Eve and the snow-covered streets throughout the town were deserted. From brightly lit windows came the tinkle of laughter and the sound of singing. The people were getting ready to welcome in the New Year. In the middle of the town square, a poor little girl was trying to make a living by selling matches. In the pocket of her old apron she carried a number of matches and she had a bundle of them in her hands. But the little match girl sat sadly beside the fountain. Her ragged dress and worn shawl could not keep out the bitter cold and she tried to keep her bare feet from touching the frozen ground.

The flakes of snow covered her long fair hair, which fell in beautiful curls around her neck, but she gave no thought to that at all. Through all the windows candles were gleaming and it smelled so deliciously of roast goose, for it was New Year's Eve and she did think about that! She had not sold any matches the whole day and she was frightened to go home, for her father would certainly be angry. It would not be much warmer anyway in the draughty old attic that was her home. The little girl's fingers were stiff with cold. If only she could light a match for some warmth! But what would her father say at such a waste!

Oh! A match might provide her a world of comfort if she only dared take a single one out of the bundle, strike it against the wall and warm her fingers by it. Falteringly she took out a match and pausing for a moment, she lit it. How it blazed and burned! It was a warm, bright flame, just like a candle. The little match girl cupped her hand over it, and as she did so, she magically saw in its light a big stove, burning brightly. The stove stood in a warm, cosy house with carpets and long red curtains. Beside the stove lay a cat with a saucer of warm milk, and in the middle of the room was a large wooden table.

On the table stood a musical box playing beautifully, and on the top of the box were a tiny boy and girl, skating hand in hand. It seemed so real to the little match girl that it was as if she was sitting before the large iron stove, with its burnished brass feet. The fire burned with such glowing warmth that it was delightful. The little girl stretched out her feet to warm them too, but the flame from the match burned out. The stove vanished, and so did the music and the skating boy and girl. The little match girl was left with only the blackened remains of the match in her hand.

The night seemed to become darker than before and it was becoming colder and colder. A shiver ran through the poor little girl's thin body. After hesitating for a long time, she finally struck another match just to have some warmth. This time, the light from the match shone brightly on the wall. The wall suddenly became transparent as if it was a veil, and the little girl could see right into a room beyond. There stood a large table, and on it was spread a tablecloth as white as the snow and a splendid porcelain dinner service. A big, roast goose lay on a plate and was steaming temptingly, with its stuffing made from apples and dried plums.

Even more wonderful still, all of a sudden the goose jumped up from the dish and danced across the table. It jumped down onto the floor and kept on dancing towards the little match girl. In fact, the whole table came alive! The little girl lifted up her nose and she could smell all of the delicious food, but then without warning, the match went out. The smell of all the food, the table, the magic porcelain dinner service and the roast goose all disappeared in an instant. Nothing was left behind, except for the cold, damp wall. Without hesitating, the girl lit another match.

This time she found herself in a room next to the most magnificent Christmas tree. The tree was filled with hundreds of small candles, glittering tinsel, tiny angels and brightly-coloured crystal balls. 'Oh, how beautiful!' exclaimed the little match girl, holding the match up in the air. Underneath the tree were presents wrapped in coloured paper with a big red ribbon around each. The tiny angels flew from the tree towards the little girl and started to sing to her. The little match girl reached out her hands to them, but right at that moment the match burned her finger and the flame flickered and then went out completely.

The lights from the Christmas tree candles flew up into the sky. Higher and higher they went, until they looked to her just like stars. Then one of the lights fell, leaving a trail behind it. Suddenly she remembered her beloved grandmother, who used to say: 'When you see a star falling, you can make a wish!' The girl quickly lit another match and the light shone round her. In the brightness stood her old grandmother, dazzling and clear, yet mild and loving in her appearance. She was in a little house with not much furniture. Next to the hearth was a small Christmas tree with some decorations and one present underneath.

'Grandmother!' cried the little match girl, 'Please take me with you. I know you will go away when the match burns out and you will vanish, just like the warm stove, the roast goose, the Christmas tree and all the other lovely things'. And without thinking twice, she rubbed the whole bundle of matches quickly against the wall to light them, as she wanted to be certain of keeping her grandmother near her. The matches gave out such a brilliant light that it was brighter than the middle of the day. Never before had her grandmother looked so beautiful and so tall. 'I wish I could be with my grandmother again forever' said the little match girl.

But this time, it was not like all the other wonderful things the poor little match girl had seen that night. Although the light from the matches faded away, her grandmother did not vanish. Instead, she remained there and gazed smiling at the little girl. Then she opened her arms and the little girl ran to her and hugged her, crying 'Granny, take me away with you please!' And with that, the grandmother took the little match girl by the hand and they walked away from the town to a better place.

At dawn the following morning, the New Year had already begun. All the people of the town were out and about celebrating the day and there was lots of singing and dancing. Meanwhile, the little match girl was with her grandmother once more, leaving nothing behind her except for one small bundle of burnt matches by the fountain. Nobody else could imagine what beautiful and magical things the little match girl had seen, or what a wonderful, bright and happy future she had entered into with her grandmother on the joyous occasion of the New Year.

The End